D0248933

THE JAZZ MAN

Woodcuts by ANN GRIFALCONI

JAZZ MAN

Mary Hays Weik

ALADDIN PAPERBACKS

Aladdin Paperbacks
An imprint of Simon & Schuster
Children's Publishing Division
1230 Avenue of the Americas
New York, NY 10020

First Aladdin Paperbacks edition 1977
Second Aladdin Paperbacks edition 1993
Printed in the United States of America
10 9 8

Library of Congress Cataloging-in-Publication Data
Weik, Mary Hays, date.
The Jazz Man / Mary Hays Weik; woodcuts by Ann Grifalconi.—
2nd Aladdin Books ed.
p. cm.
Summary: Nine-year-old Zeke, who lives in Harlem, listens to the wonderful music coming from the jazz musician's piano across the court and escapes for a while from the harsh realities that worry him.
ISBN 0-689-71767-9
[1. Jazz—Fiction. 2. Musicians—Fiction. 3. Harlem (New York, N.Y.)—Fiction. 4. Afro-Americans—Fiction.] I. Grifalconi, Ann, ill. II. Title.
PZ7.W426Jaz 1993
[Fic]—dc20 93-9965

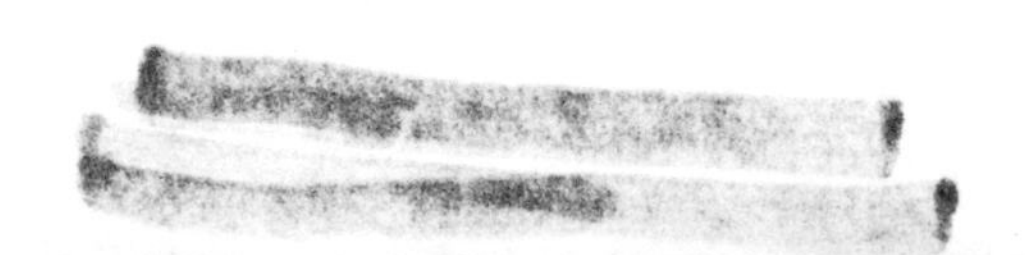

To Jennie, with love

THE JAZZ MAN

This is the story of a boy named Zeke, who lived on the topmost floor of a big old brownstone house in Harlem, U. S. A.

Zeke had not always lived there. If he shut his eyes and thought way back, he could remember a little dark house strung like a bead in a row of other little dark houses on the edge of a smoky town—and himself, Zeke, sitting hunched on a low front step, squinting his eyes to keep out the hazy sun. When he asked his Daddy where this house was, his Daddy would say "Down South, baby—where you was born, and where the band played *no* sad tunes when we-all left."

The long dark flights of stairs in the Harlem house had made Zeke's legs ache and his heart beat hot and fast when he first came to live there. That was a long time ago. The five long flights were a killer, his Daddy said. Zeke was used to them now; but they still tired out his Mama's feet, that loved to dance and run and play hop-skip games with Zeke.

At night when she came home from work, he could hear her running up the first flight: *tap, tap, tap!* Then slower: *tap—tap—tap*. Then finally the last long flight: *ta-ap . . . ta-ap . . . ta-ap*—on her little high heels, dragging up to the beatup door.

Before she opened the door, Zeke knew just what would happen. The hard thump as she dumped the big bag of groceries down on the kitchen table—as if she had had about all she could take . . . the deep breath that said *Whew.*

Then Zeke would run out from behind the door and jump up and grab her around the neck!

One of Zeke's legs was a mite shorter than the other, which gave him what his Mama called a "cute little hop step" when he walked—like a rabbit, she said smiling, making him almost proud of it. But other folks, like the kids downstairs, stared at his lame foot and made him feel hot and different. One of them even asked why he wasn't in school: how old was he? Nine, said Zeke, his heart thumping. (Why should he tell them he hid in the closet when the school man came, looking for children?) After that, he stayed upstairs in his room most of the time, and got his fun looking out of the windows.

He knew every one of the windows across the court and who lived in the rooms behind them: The clean, shiny windows with the fancy lace curtains, where cross old Mrs. Dowdy lived —old "Nasty Nice" who made her old man take off his big, muddy shoes when he came in the door, home from a long day's work in the subway tunnels . . . And the window with the crooked green blind (why *couldn't* they ever set it straight?) where Lispie—the girl who, his Daddy said, had been born, poor thing, without all her brains—sat and smiled all day and waggled her hand at him now and then . . . And the dirty, cracked window where old Bill sat and drank from his brown bottle, and shouted bad words at you if he caught you looking . . . And finally, the window that was always closed, with a brand new yellow wall inside, that looked as if it was waiting for somebody to move in and hang up pictures on it.

That window was the one Zeke watched the hardest. He kept as steady a watch on it as if he was being hired for it. It was something that could turn into almost anything, in a flash—like the tiny little box in the fairy tale, that you rubbed when you wanted something mighty nice: a carriage with six coal-black horses, or a new suit of clothes, or a turkey dinner, or a fancy cane.

An empty room with clean, new, yellow

walls—what couldn't *that* turn into? Anybody, really anybody, would be glad to move in there: a king, a bus driver, a movie star, a girl who would practice dancing steps . . . even a man with a pet monkey!

Zeke made a promise to himself—sealed in

blood from a scratch on his hand—that he would be there to see when *they* moved in, whoever they turned out to be. He stayed glued tight to his window most of every day after that, watching the empty square of yellow wall behind the closed, mysterious window. He even brought

his meals to the chair by the window—the loaf of bread and the package of ham and cheese and the little jar of mustard his Mama set out for him before she left for work—and ate his sandwiches as he watched. Nobody was there to see him at it, except Lispie (who didn't care) and old Bill, who never saw anything but his bottle anyway.

For a long time, the yellow room just sat there by itself. Waiting. Maybe waiting for *nobody*, Zeke thought sometimes, getting sadder and sadder! But one day, when he had almost given up hope, it happened. The yellow room came to life. Zeke saw two men set down a big brown box in front of the closed window. His heart jumped as he waited for a little door to open in the side and the monkey to peer out. But the men went away, and no door opened, no monkey looked out: the long brown box stood still.

Then a big dark hand, that he somehow liked, reached out and unlocked the window, pushed up the sash. A friendly face looked out at him—"Hi, boy!"

"Hi!" said Zeke softly.

The man disappeared. When he came back, he dragged a chair with him that he set down in front of the big box. He took off his coat and rolled up his shirt-sleeves carefully, and sat down with his back to the open window. Zeke watched him turn a key in the front of the box and fold back a long shelf that ran across the middle. Now

comes the monkey, thought Zeke, hopping up and down with excitement.

But all he saw uncovered was a long strip of shiny black and white. The man stroked his hand across it as if he loved it. He tapped it softly and a sound like a bell—only nicer than a bell—came out. He spread his big fingers across it and the thing in the box began to sing: to cry like a lonesome child at night, to talk to Zeke about all the things that nobody in the world had ever talked to him about before, that explained everything that had ever happened in his whole life.

"He is what you would call a Jazz Man, baby," Zeke's Daddy told him that night. "That thing he is playing is a piano, and what it says is strictly between it and him and you."

Real music, the real *business*: that was what his Daddy meant, Zeke knew, and it pleased him to have him agree with what he, Zeke, had already decided.

After that the two of them, Zeke and his Daddy, would sit in the dark and listen to the Jazz Man playing. And Zeke's Mama, when she came in late from work and bumped the groceries down on the kitchen table, would kick off her high-heeled shoes and sit and listen too. So then there were three of them sitting there in the dark, close together, listening, and Zeke was as happy as any boy could be.

It seemed to Zeke after that that they lived in a new and wonderful world. The tall old brownstone house seemed to reach up and touch the sky, and the swing and flow of the Jazz Man's music wrapped them all around in a happiness that would surely last forever.

It was funny the way he never seemed to get tired of playing—just as you never got tired of listening to him. Soft and smooth was the way he played, so that something inside you reached out and asked for more. He didn't seem to need to eat or sleep. Sometimes he looked almost as big as God. Sometimes he was as little and weak and crazy as you were—and his music crept off till you could hardly hear it. Then it would pick up the beat again and come back, full and hot and strong.

It was wonderful what he could do. He could play a table of food right down in front of you when you were hungry. He could play your Mama's worries right out of her head, when the rent man was nagging her for the rent money she didn't have. He could play the sad look off her mouth, and shiny silver slippers onto her feet—just like that!—and zip her into a party dress with silver stars all over it, smelling of violet perfume (the kind she loved!), and start her dancing like she used to do.

He could play your Daddy out of his no-job blues, play the dreams right out of his old brown bottle, and make him feel like the king of the universe.

And sometimes on a hot night, when the jiggety street lights burned in your eyes, and you, Zeke, lay there awake, he could play the big cool shadows down around you . . .

Till the drippy faucet sounded like a tiny little waterfall in the jungle.

And the roar of the subway under the street was the roar of an African lion, the king of the jungle himself, calling goodnight to the little jungle beasts hid in the trailing trees.

And the chatter of the windows as the train roared past was the chatter of the monkeys hanging in the trees, calling a friendly goodnight right back to old king Lion.

And the rumble of the city was the wind in the jungle trees.

And the smoke and smell of the city was the steamy jungle blackness

that folded around you like a friendly coat and drifted you off to sleep.

There were other days that seemed like a wonderful party—a party where Zeke was always welcome, though he never once stepped into the yellow room. That was when the Jazz Man's friends came in for a session: Tony and Ernie and little Manuel. (These were the names Zeke's Daddy gave them.) They had to come to the Jazz Man's place, for *he* had the piano, and that was too big to carry anywhere.

What a time they had! They usually played all day and half the night. There was Tony,

Italian, with a laughing red mouth, who played a silver trumpet, high and sweet.

And big black Ernie, who (Zeke's Daddy said) made soft love with his saxophone.

And Manuel, who was Puerto Rican and got so happy when he played his drums that he flung the sticks around like crazy.

And the Jazz Man just sat there and played and played, and laughed at all of them with his white teeth shining.

When they saw Zeke watching out of his window, they would laugh out loud and wave him a friendly hello. Tony would blow him a special note on his silver trumpet, soft and sweet, and Ernie would waggle his sax at him. And the Jazz Man would look back over his shoulder and smile and play right on—just as Zeke hoped he would.

The hot summer drifted on and on, and just when you thought it would last forever, it was gone, in a flurry of chill days. Open windows began to come down. Lispie's mother folded a sweater around her as she sat at the window, and Zeke could hear old Bill across the court, coughing in his bed.

The long stairs to the street were no chore for Zeke now. When he went downstairs—which was not so often—he hopped up two, three, four, five flights like a rabbit. But his Mama never seemed to get used to them. She hated them more every day.

She hated the kind of jobs Zeke's Daddy got, too. He liked jobs with life and movement in them—driving trucks, or running elevators, or following the races. But somehow his jobs always led him into trouble. The trucks he drove were always smashing into something. The elevators he ran got stuck in between floors, and then he was usually fired. And the races . . . well, he came home broke from almost every one.

"I just don't understand," Zeke's Mama would say. "Other men got steady jobs."

"Like what?"

"Like waiting table, with fancy tips."

"Those other men ain't me," his Daddy would tell her. "As a waiter man I am strictly no good. If you think you would like those other men better, you know what to do, baby."

She knew all right. One night she held Zeke in her lap for a long time. She was teaching him

how to read. They read the same story over together, twice. When he leaned against her cheek it was wet; and she rocked him to sleep like she had when he was a baby. He was still asleep when she went off to work next morning. He got up and made his breakfast, and ate it alone. All day long he told himself she would come home sure enough at night, sang crazy songs to himself, and made up stories about the folks he could see walking like ants in the court below his window.

When it began to get dark he got behind the door, waiting to jump out at her when she came in, loaded with groceries. But all the time he knew deep down inside she wouldn't come. Finally when all the street lights had come on and the juke-box in the tavern across the street had opened up full blast, he came out from behind the door, found a piece of ham in the icebox, made a sandwich, and went to bed.

"You and me," said his Daddy, "has got to learn how to cook." They tried too, and at first it was like old times, when they had first moved into the Harlem house and *she* was there. Zeke's Daddy would stick a high paper hat on his head like a chef, and Zeke would giggle and set the table, and in no time at all his Daddy would open up a few cans and have a fancy meal on the table.

But after a while his Daddy began to forget to come home for supper. He was sorry, Zeke

knew, when he came home late with a bottle tucked under his arm, and found him, Zeke, in bed. He would stand there over the bed looking down at Zeke without a word. And the trouble in him would soak down into Zeke, lying very still and pretending to be asleep so as not to embarrass him.

Time came when Zeke's Daddy stayed away from home for days. When there was food in the icebox sometimes and sometimes hardly any at all. And Zeke got quieter and skinnier than ever. He seldom went to the door any more when someone knocked—even if it was food they might be bringing him. People were apt to ask questions.

"Where has your Mama gone?" they would ask—looking at him sideways with eyes that said: "*We* know and *you* know she won' come back!"

"She's gone on a trip!" Zeke would say quickly, "A long way off—to my rich Auntie's!"

"Rich Auntie better send you some rent," they would answer, their noses up in the air, "And some stuff to eat, too. Can't expect *us* to go on forever carrying food up here for you—telling the landlord big tales he don' believe. We got families of our own."

"You wait," Zeke would tell them, feeling his heart sink lower and lower. "She'll come back all right—and bring presents for you and everybody!"

But he knew—and they knew—it was all in his mind: rich Auntie and presents and all. His Mama was gone. She had rocked him to sleep, and gone away. Where? How would he find her?

Maybe his Daddy knew . . . But he was gone too. Where *that* man was (Zeke heard them say) was anybody's guess. Could be in jail.

"Just no good, the two of 'em!" they said, loud enough for Zeke to hear. He made up his mind then. When they went away, he took the food they had brought him and set it carefully outside the door, in the hall. Then he shut the door and locked it.

Did you ever wake up in the night, all of a sudden, when everyone else is asleep and the street outside is as still as death? Have you ever seen the moon stare down out of a frozen sky on a world where nobody else is alive but you?

Zeke woke that night to such a world. For what seemed years he lay there shivering, staring into the inky shadows that crept across the room. Then suddenly down below, with a wild clatter of garbage cans, a wind swept through the narrow court, and the tall old building shook and the floors trembled. Zeke was afraid and pulled the covers up over his head. He tried to remember the stories his Mama had told him, about the jokes the wind likes to play on scaredy-cats. But somehow it didn't seem funny any more, lying there all alone.

Suddenly he sat straight up in bed, remem-

bering that for days now he had heard no sound from the Jazz Man's room across the court. In his worrying over his Mama and Daddy, he had clean forgot the Jazz Man and his friends! He jumped out of bed and ran to the window.

The room across the court was dark. The window blind was pulled down and everything was as still as still could be. The Jazz Man had gone away too . . .

Zeke lay in bed with his eyes closed tight, trying to think of something besides the hungry ache inside him, something warm and cozy . . . If he *had* a rich Auntie, now: what would she look like? Tall and skinny; or round and fluffy-haired, with a soft lap to sit on? Probably round, he decided, if she was rich—because then she would not have to work hard and wear herself thin, like the women downstairs. But even rich people liked to cook sometimes. And for Zeke, her sweetie-pie, what wouldn't his Auntie make —cookies, cakes, tarts, meat loaf, strawberry puddings . . . The thought was too much for him. He jumped out of bed and ran to the kitchen. The icebox door stood open—in the moonlight, he could see its empty shelves. But there was still the cupboard. He pulled up a chair and climbed onto the kitchen table, to look on the topmost shelf of the tall cupboard. But all he found was an old box of toothpicks, covered with last year's dust.

Slowly Zeke climbed down and turned back to bed. He was cold now—as cold as could be—

and he pulled down the covers of the bed and crawled back between the wrinkled sheets, shivering; made a wooly nest in the blankets to keep warm. After a while he dropped off to sleep.

It was still dark, pitchy-dark, when Zeke sat up in bed with a start, convinced that the Jazz Man was back—his mind so full of the music of piano and horn and drum and sax that he had to run over to the window and see for himself if they had really come back.

But they hadn't. The blind was still down, and the window to the Jazz Man's room was shut as tight as ever, as tight as death. Slowly Zeke turned away. Cold as his own room was, his head felt hot and dizzy. The ache in his chest still hurt. He put on his clothes, feeling shaky and weak, and opened the door to the hall. Holding on tight to the stair-rail, he started down the stairs. After a million years, he reached the street.

The wind had quieted down. It was starting

to drizzle: a thin light rain that made the streets shiny and black, painted them with a witch's carpet of dancing colored lights. Zeke held onto the damp brick walls of the buildings as he went along, feeling as if his feet belonged to somebody else. For the life of him, he couldn't remember where it was he was going.

He was trying to find somebody—just who, he didn't know. Somebody he knew better than himself. Who knew all about him too—who he was, what he looked like, how mixed-up he was. And who still loved him.

Thinking about it, his head felt lighter. The hurt was still inside his chest, but he felt bigger, stronger, braver. Letting go of the brick wall, he decided to cross the street, to where on the opposite corner red and green lights were winking off and on at him, and more lights, warm and inviting, were shining out of a tavern window.

Carefully he crossed the black, slippery street, keeping an eye on the green traffic light as his Mama had taught him. The glittery shades were

down on the tavern windows, but a soft and golden glow came through, and Zeke peered under an open corner to see the room inside.

The place shone like a party with lights and music. Zeke held his breath as he watched. Could it be true? Across the room, hazy with smoke and crowded with tables and smiling, dressed-up people, was the Jazz Man, playing on a gold piano and nodding his big head to the beat! And

there was Tony too, standing beside him on the little platform, making his silver trumpet laugh, and Manuel with his crazy drums, and Ernie waggling his sax like an elephant's golden trunk!

Someone opened the door beside Zeke, a man and a girl. Taking a quick, deep breath, Zeke slipped in after them. A smell of violets, and a grand hot smell of food rose up to meet him—roast ham and turkey and candied yams and everything he most loved. Zeke drew a quick, hot breath and stopped dead still. What did it mean? Everyone in the big, warm, shining, friendly room—the waiters in their sharp black suits, the dressed-up men and women, even the Jazz Man and his friends—was standing up and looking at him, Zeke, as if they had all been waiting for him and he was a king!

It was wonderful; but the hurt in his chest was still there. Zeke reached across to his other arm and took a quick hard pinch of his brown skin . . .

"What for you pinch yourself, boy?"

It was his Daddy's voice! Zeke looked up from where he was lying, scrooched up in his own bed, and there was his Daddy, looking down at him, a strange shine in his eyes.

"Look what I brought you, baby," he said. And there, slipping out from behind the door, with a funny little tearful smile on her face, was Zeke's Mama, as big as life.